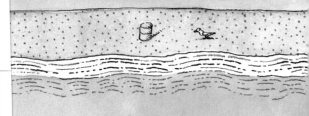

JUV/E    Sis, Peter.
FIC
        Beach ball.

$13.00

| DATE | | | |
|---|---|---|---|
| | | | |
| | | | |
| | | | |
| | | | |
| | | | |
| | | | |
| | | | |
| | | | |
| | | | |
| | | | |
| | | | |
| | | | |

BAKER & TAYLOR

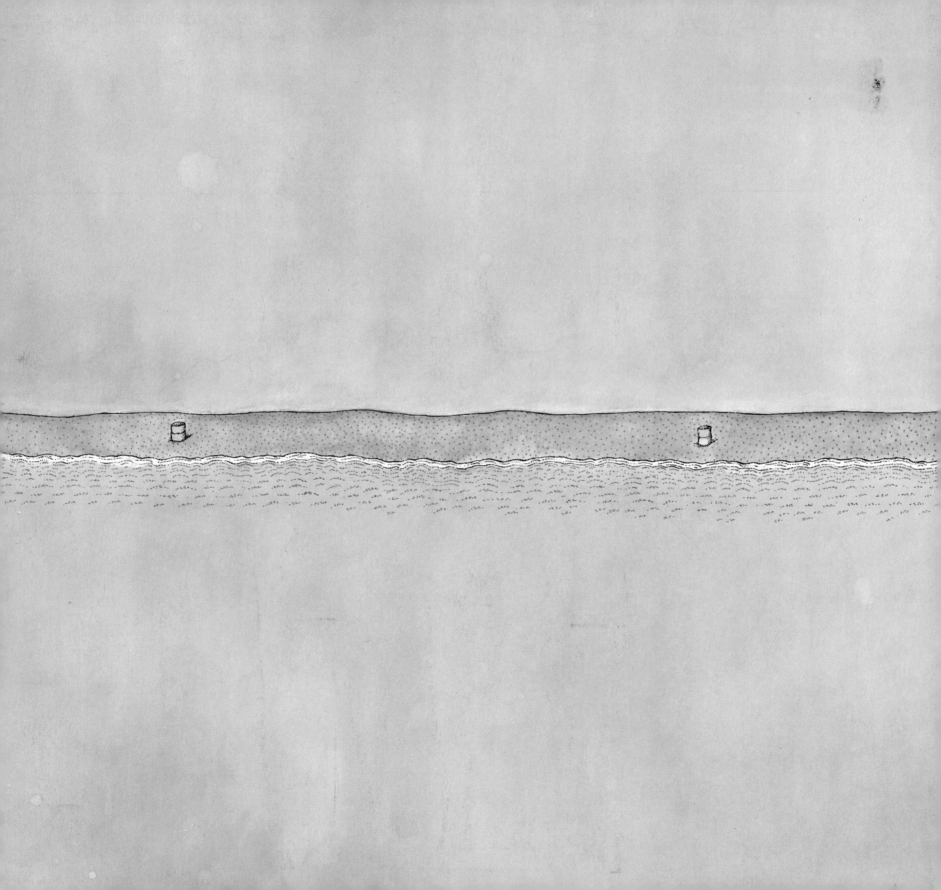

# Beach Ball

## by PETER SIS

GREENWILLOW BOOKS, New York

For my landlocked sister Hana,
who loves beaches

Pen and ink and watercolor paints were used for the full-color art.
Copyright © 1990 by Peter Sis. All rights reserved. No part of this
book may be reproduced or utilized in any form or by any means, electronic
or mechanical, including photocopying, recording, or by any
information storage and retrieval system, without permission in writing
from the Publisher, Greenwillow Books, a division of William Morrow
& Company, Inc., 105 Madison Avenue, New York, NY 10016.
Printed in Singapore by Tien Wah Press
First Edition  10 9 8 7 6 5 4 3 2

Library of Congress Cataloging-in-Publication Data
Sis, Peter.
Beach ball / Peter Sis.    p.    cm.
Summary: While at the beach, Mary and her mother see
letters, numbers, colors, shapes, and more.
ISBN 0-688-09181-4. ISBN 0-688-09182-2 (lib. bdg.)
[1. Beaches—Fiction.      2. Mothers and daughters—Fiction.]
I. Title.    PZ7.S6219At  1990    [E]—dc19    89-2076    CIP    AC

# THE WIND BLEW MARY'S BALL AWAY

ABCDEFGHIJKLMNOPQ

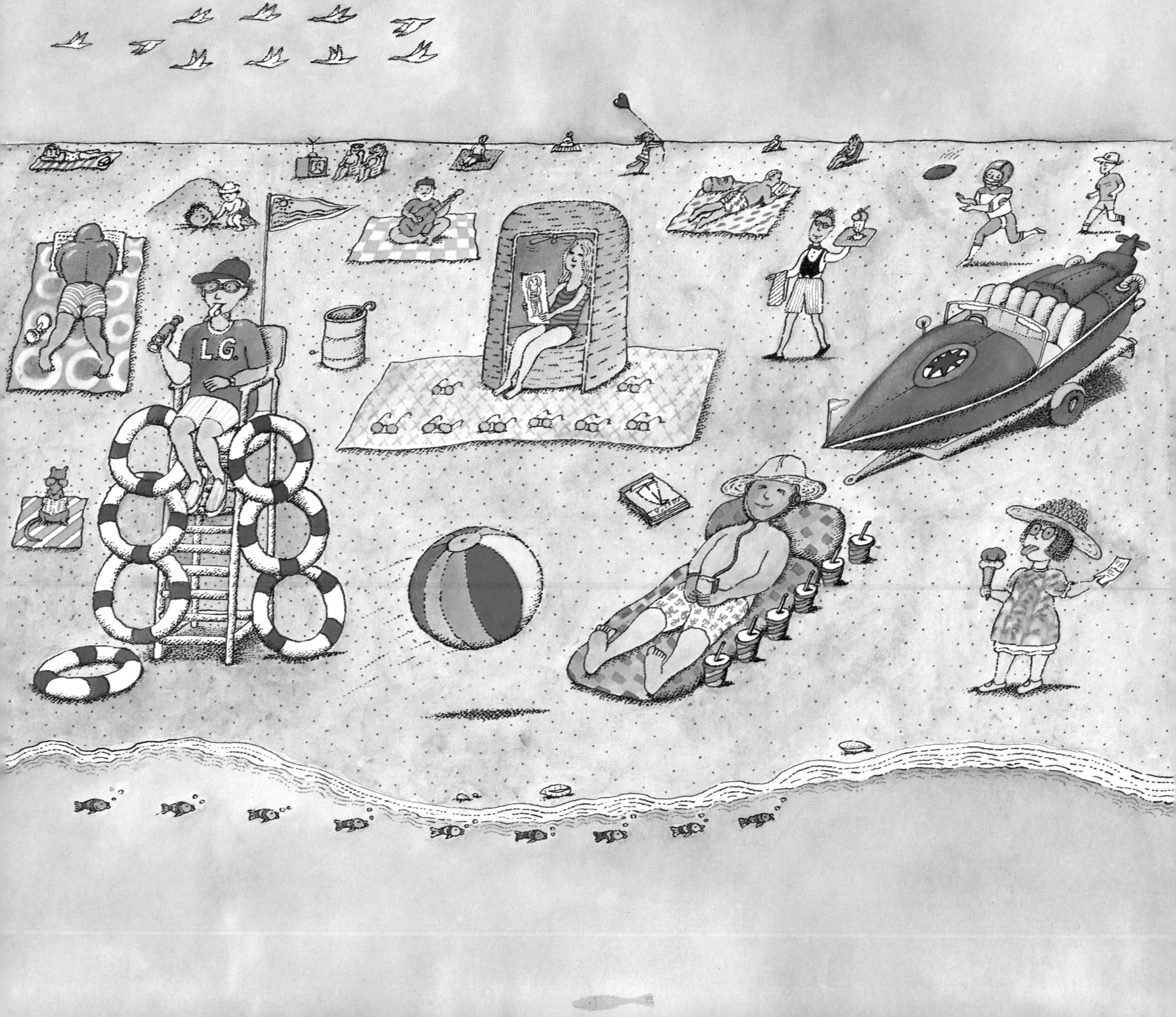
L.G.

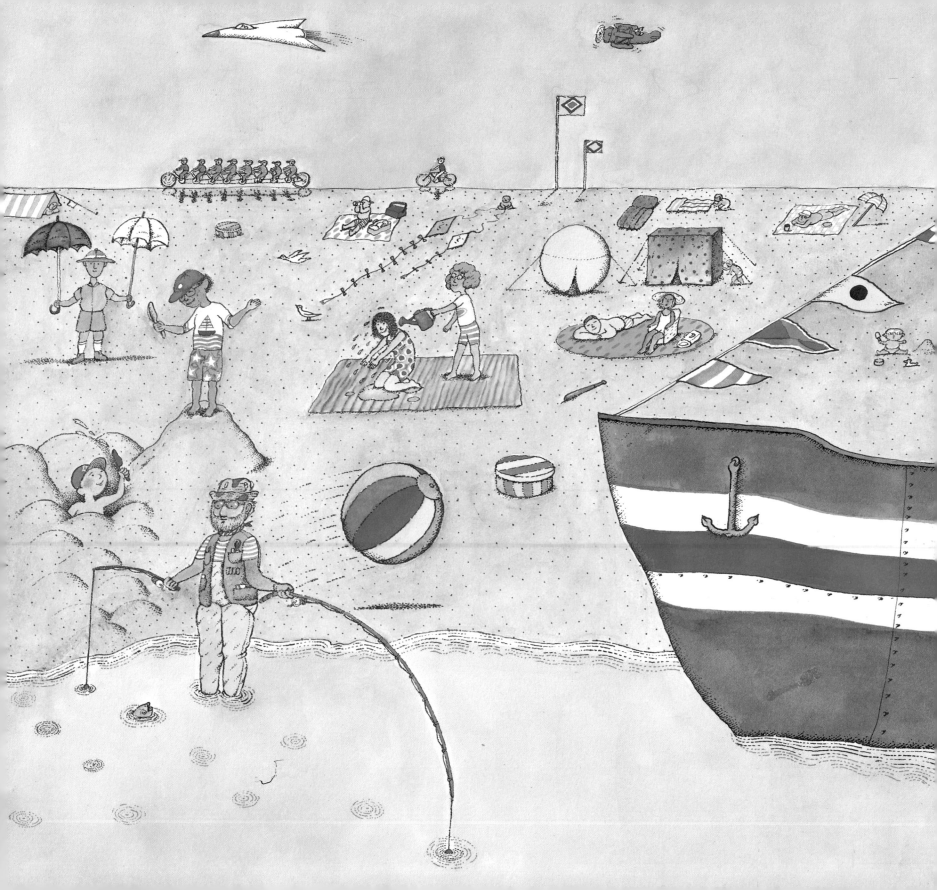

# NAME THE ANIMALS